PERSPECTIVES FLIP BOOK

The Split History of the

CIVIL WAR

UNION PERSPECTIVE

BY STEPHANIE FITZGERALD

CONTENT CONSULTANT:
Mark Snell, PhD
Professor of History/Director
George Tyler Moore Center for the Study of the Civil War
Shepherd University

COMPASS POINT BOOKS
a capstone imprint

Compass Point Books
1710 Roe Crest Drive
North Mankato, Minnesota 56003
www.capstonepub.com

Library of Congress Cataloging-in-Publication Data
Fitzgerald, Stephanie.
  The split history of the Civil War : a perspectives flip book / by Stephanie Fitzgerald.
     pages cm. — (Perspectives flip book)
  Includes bibliographical references and index.
  Summary: "Describes the opposing viewpoints of the North and South during the American Civil
War"—Provided by publisher.
  ISBN 978-0-7565-4572-7 (library binding)
  ISBN 978-0-7565-4594-9 (paperback)
  ISBN 978-0-7565-4630-4 (ebook PDF)
  1. United States—History—Civil War, 1861-1865—Juvenile literature. I. Title.
  E468.F564 2013
  973—dc23   2012004680

EDITOR
ANGIE KAELBERER

DESIGNER
ASHLEE SUKER

MEDIA RESEARCHER
WANDA WINCH

LIBRARY CONSULTANT
KATHLEEN BAXTER

PRODUCTION SPECIALIST
MICHELLE BIEDSCHEID

IMAGE CREDITS
Union Perspective: Appomattox Court House National Historical Park, 28; Bridgeman Art Library:
©Chicago History Museum, USA/Paul Phillipoteaux, 11; Courtesy of Army Art Collection, U.S. Army
Center of Military History, 18; Library of Congress: Prints and Photographs Division, 5, 6, 12, 23, 25;
National Archives and Records Administration (NARA): Mathew Brady Collection, 26; National Parks
Service: Antietam National Battlefield, Maryland, 15; www.historicalimagebank.com, painting by Don
Trioani, cover (all), 8

Confederate Perspective: Alamy: Everett Collection Inc., 27, North Wind Picture Archives, 23;
Bridgeman Art Library: ©Look and Learn/Private Collection/Angus McBride, 17; National Archives
and Records Administration (NARA), 26, Matthew Brady Collection, 5, 12, Timothy O'Sullivan, 24,
28; SuperStock Inc: Pantheon, 15; www.historicalimagebank.com, painting by Don Troiani, cover
(all), 8, 10,18, 21

Art elements: Shutterstock: Color Symphony, paper texture, Ebtikar, flag, Sandra Cunningham,
grunge photo, SvetlanaR, grunge lines

Printed in China by Nordica.
1114/CA21401818
112014   008621R

Table of Contents

CH. i 1861: INSURRECTION!

*B*oom!

At 4:30 in the morning April 12, 1861, residents of Charleston,

South Carolina, awoke to the sound of cannons. The cannons in

Charleston Harbor were firing upon a U.S. Army fort. But the

attack on Fort Sumter didn't come from a foreign country. The

soldiers firing the cannons were Americans—U.S. citizens who had

left their country to found another one. The attack continued for

34 hours before the U.S. soldiers at the fort surrendered. The

United States was now involved in a civil war.

Upon winning independence from Great Britain in 1783, the

United States became one country. But that didn't mean that

Confederate soldiers fired on Fort Sumter April 12, 1861.

everyone in the nation agreed on important issues. By 1860 issues concerning the spread of slavery into the western territories of the country divided the northern and southern states.

The nation's 34 states were more different than similar. The South's dependence on slave labor caused political, economic, social, and cultural disagreements that tore the country apart.

The northern economy was based on industry, although it also outproduced the South in agriculture. There were more than five times as many factories in the North than in the South. The North also boasted a growing population, thanks to the constant addition of European immigrants. The economy did not rely on slave labor, and it was outlawed in many places. People in the North didn't want slavery spreading to new states as they were added to the Union.

Lincoln took office March 4, 1861.

Southern states had talked about secession for years. The Republican political party was determined to stop the spread of slavery. When northern Republican candidate Abraham Lincoln won the presidential election in November 1860, the die was cast. South Carolina left the Union before the year was over.

By the time Lincoln was inaugurated March 4, 1861, six more states had seceded to form the Confederate States of America: Alabama, Florida, Georgia, Louisiana, Mississippi, and Texas. Jefferson Davis was named president of the Confederacy.

Lincoln tried to reassure those angered by his election. In his inaugural address, he stated that he would not endanger "their property, and their peace and personal security." But he also made it clear that he would not accept dissolution of the Union.

Within a week after the attack on Fort Sumter, Virginia seceded from the Union. Arkansas, North Carolina, and Tennessee soon followed Virginia.

SETTING THE STAGE FOR WAR

After the attack on Fort Sumter, Lincoln called for 75,000 volunteers to put down the insurrection. Those who answered the call felt a patriotic duty to protect their country and preserve the Union. Most were not fighting to end slavery.

In May Richmond, Virginia, was named the Confederate capital. Northerners urged Lincoln to strike Richmond immediately to crush the rebellion. Though his troops weren't ready, Lincoln attempted to do just that.

When General Irvin McDowell explained that the army wasn't prepared, Lincoln responded, "Your men are green, it is true, but they (the Confederates) are green also; you are all green alike." There had been minor skirmishes during the first three months of the war. Now McDowell was about to lead his inexperienced men into their first major battle.

THE FIRST BATTLE OF BULL RUN

In mid-July McDowell began moving his troops from Alexandria, Virginia, toward the railroad junction at the town of Manassas, the best overland route into the Confederate capital. On July 18

Union soldiers, wearing the red uniforms of their regiment, fought the Confederate cavalry at Bull Run.

McDowell reached Centreville, about 5 miles (8 kilometers) from a little stream called Bull Run. He knew he would have to cross the stream, but it was guarded by Confederate troops under the command of General Pierre G.T. Beauregard.

Union troops attacked the Confederates but were soon driven back. When the main battle occurred July 21, the Union army at first managed to push back the enemy troops. Southern soldiers were fleeing in confusion when Confederate General Thomas Jackson and his troops joined the fight. Their support helped the Confederates regain their position and earned Jackson and his brigade the nickname of "Stonewall."

Late in the day the Confederates made a counterattack that sent the Union troops running from the field. People who had come to watch the fight—northern politicians and civilians who treated the spectacle as a picnic—fled in panic and confusion. The Union army lost the battle and about 2,900 men who were killed, wounded, or missing. For the first time people realized there would not be a quick end to the war.

Soon after the defeat at Bull Run, Lincoln replaced McDowell with General George McClellan. The president would eventually regret his choice.

BULL RUN VS. MANASSAS

The Union usually named battles after the closest river or stream. The Confederates usually named battles after railroad junctions or towns. That's why the North refers to this battle as Bull Run, and in the South it is known as Manassas. Other Civil War battles went by different names in the North and South. They included Antietam, called Sharpsburg in the South, and Shiloh, known as Pittsburg Landing in the North.

CH. 2 1862: GRIM REALITY

*N*early 200,000 new volunteers poured into Washington following the bitter defeat at Bull Run. General McClellan trained and drilled the recruits in the hopes of preventing another defeat.

Meanwhile, General Ulysses S. Grant was taking action in the West. He captured Fort Henry on the Tennessee River February 6, 1862. Then he turned east to Fort Donelson on the Cumberland River. That fort fell February 16. Two of the major water transportation routes in the Confederate West were now in the hands of the Union.

The Union capture of Fort Donelson led to the fall of Nashville, Tennessee.

The victory forced General Albert Sidney Johnston, head of the Confederacy's Western Department, to evacuate Nashville, Tennessee. General Beauregard was transferred from Virginia to act as Johnston's second-in-command. His forces were to join Johnston's at a railroad connection at Corinth, Mississippi.

BATTLE OF PITTSBURG LANDING (SHILOH)

Grant established his camp just northeast of the Confederates in Corinth, at a place called Pittsburg Landing, Tennessee. Then he waited for reinforcements from the Army of the Ohio under General Don Carlos Buell.

The Confederate attack arrived before Buell did, the morning of April 6. For 12 hours the Union troops were battered, bloodied, and pushed from their positions. Still Grant would not give up. "Well, General, we've had the devil's own day of it, haven't we?" remarked General William Tecumseh Sherman. "Yes," Grant responded. "Lick 'em tomorrow, though."

The following morning the Union army, armed with fresh reinforcements, attacked. After several hours of fighting and heavy losses, Beauregard and his troops retreated to Corinth. Johnston had been killed the first day of the battle.

The narrow victory for the Union came at a terrible price. More than 13,000 soldiers were dead, missing, or injured. The

The Union won the Battle of Pittsburg Landing, but at a great cost.

Confederates suffered losses of about 10,000. The incredible carnage of the two-day battle shocked the nation. Many demanded that Grant be relieved of command. "I can't spare this man," President Lincoln said. "He fights."

In the East Lincoln was relying on a general who *didn't* always fight. George McClellan preferred to avoid bloodshed if he could. He also worried about being outnumbered by the Confederates. "If we had a million men, McClellan would swear the enemy has two millions," complained Secretary of War Edwin Stanton. "And then he would sit down in the mud and yell for three."

By June 1 McClellan was just a few miles away from Richmond. But rather than attacking, McClellan had his men dig in—despite the fact that he had more than twice the number of men the Confederates did. The fight was finally brought to McClellan June 26. Troops under Confederate General Robert E. Lee, who assumed command after General Joseph Johnston was wounded, attacked the Union soldiers. After a week of fighting, called the Seven Days' Battles, the Union soldiers retreated from Richmond. With almost 16,000 men killed, missing, or wounded, the North suffered fewer casualties than the South. But once again, an opportunity to capture the Confederate capital had been lost.

SECOND BATTLE OF BULL RUN

Within a month, fighting shifted to northern Virginia. The evening of August 28 General Stonewall Jackson led a brief attack on Union troops near Manassas Junction. The next day Union General John

Pope attacked Jackson's troops. The Union vastly outnumbered the Confederates, and as the day ended, seemed to have victory in hand.

Confederate reinforcements arrived later that day, though, commanded by General James Longstreet. The next afternoon Longstreet's forces launched a surprise attack. The Union line was shattered and forced to retreat, with about 14,500 casualties. The defeat was a terrible blow to the North. Pope's Army of Virginia was combined with McClellan's Army of the Potomac, under McClellan's overall command.

THE BATTLE OF ANTIETAM

Emboldened by the victory at Manassas, General Lee began a northern invasion into Maryland in September. McClellan, once again in charge, led the Army of the Potomac to meet the enemy.

Luck appeared to be on McClellan's side. He acquired a copy of Lee's battle plan and learned that Lee had divided his army. On September 14 McClellan and Lee's troops fought at South Mountain, near Frederick, Maryland. The Union troops beat back the Confederates, who planned to retreat to Virginia. But Lee changed his mind after hearing that Stonewall Jackson had captured the Union garrison at Harper's Ferry, Virginia. Lee set up a defensive line on the high ground near Antietam Creek and waited for McClellan to arrive.

At dawn September 17, thousands of blue-coated soldiers faced Lee's army across Antietam Creek. Savage fighting raged across the battlefield all day. Despite heavy losses on both sides, neither army

Union General Ambrose Burnside led the capture of the bridge over Antietam Creek.

backed down. By the end of the day, Union casualties numbered about 12,000 and Confederate around 11,000, earning it the name "the bloodiest single day in American history." Lee retreated to Virginia the evening of September 18. McClellan sent a division after him, but those soldiers were defeated September 20 at the Battle of Shepherdstown.

The tactical Union victory gave Lincoln the chance he had been waiting for to issue the preliminary Emancipation Proclamation. It gave notice that if the Confederates had not rejoined the Union by January 1, 1863, the slaves in Confederate states would be freed. Before that would happen, though, the Union would suffer its worst defeat so far at Fredericksburg, Virginia.

THE BATTLE OF FREDERICKSBURG

In November General Ambrose Burnside was named commander
of the Army of the Potomac — the main eastern Union army.
On December 13 he set out to attack Lee's forces, which were
amassed near Fredericksburg on high ground that included a ridge
called Marye's Heights.

Lee's troops held a strong position on Marye's Heights. The men
were lined up four-deep behind a shoulder-high stone wall at the
end of an open field. Nevertheless, Burnside sent wave after wave of
troops at the wall. One after the other, the soldiers were cut down
by continuous fire from the Confederates. Not one man made it to
the wall. Union troops fared somewhat better a few miles to the
south, but still lost the battle, with casualties of about 12,500.

The demoralized Union army retired to its winter quarters
near Falmouth, Virginia. General Joseph Hooker was named as
Burnside's replacement. He set about reorganizing his troops and
improving their spirits. He knew he would need his army at its best
for the battles to come.

LEE'S "LOST ORDER"

Robert E. Lee's Special Order No. 191, which
detailed his plan for the northern invasion,
was discovered by two Union soldiers, who found
it wrapped around three cigars that a careless
Confederate officer had dropped. When McClellan
read the order he said, "Here is a paper with
which, if I cannot whip Bobby Lee, I will be
willing to go home."

1863:
A BLOODY STRUGGLE

Vicksburg, Mississippi, was a heavily defended town high on a bluff on the eastern bank of the Mississippi River. Guns pointed down on a 5-mile (8-km) stretch of the river. Heavily forested swamps protected the overland approaches to the north and south. It would not be an easy assault, but it was crucial. If the Union gained control over the entire Mississippi River, the eastern Confederate states would be cut off from Louisiana, Arkansas, and Texas—and the important supplies they provided.

General Grant was in charge of the Vicksburg campaign. Grant tried a number of tactics before setting on a bold and dangerous plan. He would march his army along the western shore of the Mississippi to a point south of Vicksburg. Under the cover of night, Admiral David Dixon Porter would sail his riverboat fleet down the river to meet Grant's men and ferry them to the other side.

At the end of April, Grant moved his 50,000 troops across the river. They then marched eastward, took the capital of Mississippi at Jackson, and marched west toward Vicksburg. By May 18 they managed to force the Confederates back to Vicksburg and began a siege of the city. After six weeks of constant bombardment—and near starvation—Vicksburg finally surrendered July 4, 1863.

Union troops attacked Vicksburg in 1863 before laying siege to the city.

THE BATTLE OF CHANCELLORSVILLE

The appointment of General Hooker gave the men of the Army of the Potomac a morale boost that they badly needed. The general, nicknamed "Fighting Joe," had a reputation as a good soldier and leader. To decrease desertion, he started revolving furloughs for the men. He also made sure that his troops received better rations. This improved the soldiers' health and helped swell the ranks of his command with new enlistees. Hooker now commanded about 130,000 men.

Toward the end of April, he chose to prove his might against the Army of Northern Virginia by striking at Fredericksburg. "My plans are perfect," Hooker bragged, "and when I start to carry them out may God have mercy on General Lee, for I will have none."

Hooker's plan may have been "perfect," but it didn't fool Lee. Hooker sent three corps downstream on the Rappahannock River to divert Lee's attention. By April 30 Hooker had his headquarters—and 70,000 men—set up 10 miles (16 km) west of Fredericksburg at a crossroads called Chancellorsville. But Lee figured out what Hooker was doing. Instead of retreating, he moved toward Hooker's forces. The morning of May 1, Hooker marched his troops eastward through dense forests called the Wilderness, coming near the Confederate forces before retreating to Chancellorsville.

The evening of May 2, Confederate troops under General Stonewall Jackson burst through the Wilderness and attacked Hooker's men. The fighting continued for two days before Hooker led a full retreat, taking his troops north of the Rappahannock. He had lost a staggering 17,000 soldiers.

The defeat sent shock waves through the North. Once again Lincoln had to find a replacement general for the Army of the Potomac. By the end of June he had replaced Hooker with Major General George Gordon Meade. A few days later Meade led his men north into Pennsylvania. Lee meant to press his advantage after Chancellorsville by invading the North. Meade would have to stop him.

GETTYSBURG

The Union cavalry under General John Buford reached Gettysburg, Pennsylvania, June 30—just slightly ahead of the Confederates. Buford quickly took the high ground at a spot called McPherson's Ridge, just west of town. The cavalry encountered Confederate soldiers under Brigadier General James Pettigrew, but the Confederates quickly retreated. The night of June 30, Buford's scouts reported several Confederate encampments nearby. Buford knew that a battle was soon coming.

That battle began with a shot fired by one of Buford's troops about 7:30 the morning of July 1. Between 8 and 9 a.m., the fighting began in earnest. Buford's men managed to hold off a Confederate attack while Union reinforcements rushed to the scene. As thousands of Union and Confederate soldiers joined the fight, the Confederates seemed to gain the advantage. The Union forces were slowly being pushed back through Gettysburg.

THE MASSACHUSETTS 54TH

With the Emancipation Proclamation of January 1, 1863, Lincoln announced that African-American men would be accepted into the U.S. Army. About 180,000 answered the call. One of the best-known regiments of black soldiers was the 54th Massachusetts Volunteer Infantry Regiment. It gained fame for leading the July 18, 1863, assault on Fort Wagner in South Carolina. The regiment's story was told in the 1989 movie *Glory.*

Union General Meade arrived by midnight, along with troops that would ultimately number about 93,000. The men eventually would be deployed in a line 3 miles (4.8 km) long on the high ground outside of town. The Confederates attacked the afternoon of July 2. Throughout several hours of brutal fighting, the Union lines managed to hold, but just barely.

Meade's army remained dug in along Cemetery Ridge to protect their position atop Cemetery Hill, managing to hold off a Confederate assault. On July 3 the Confederates staged a massive charge, with about 12,000 men advancing on Cemetery Ridge. Union cannons blasted them as they charged, resulting in casualties of more than half the force. At the cost of about 23,000 casualties in its army, the Union had won the battle of Gettysburg—and turned the tide of the war in the East.

CH.4 1864–1865:

MARCH TO VICTORY

In March 1864 General Ulysses Grant was made supreme commander of all the Union armies. Lincoln finally had a leader who understood how to win the war. Grant wasn't interested in conquering cities—he was interested in conquering armies. And the two strongest Confederate armies left were Lee's Army of Northern Virginia and the Army of Tennessee, under the command of Joseph E. Johnston.

When Grant took his post, he turned over command of the Army of the West to General William Tecumseh Sherman. Sherman's orders were to move toward Atlanta to engage and defeat the

General Ulysses Grant gained a reputation as a tough, steadfast fighter.

Army of Tennessee. At the same time, the Army of the Potomac would move toward Richmond to draw Lee into a fight.

The operation began May 4, with Grant accompanying General Meade and the Army of the Potomac across the Rapidan River in northern Virginia. Grant's goal was to reach the open country south of the river and engage Lee's army there. Lee had other ideas.

BATTLE OF THE WILDERNESS

Confederates attacked the Union troops May 5 as they marched through the Wilderness, near the old Chancellorsville battle site. Private Warren Goss of the 2nd Massachusetts Artillery described the scene: "No one could see the fight fifty feet from him. The roll and crackle of the musketry was something terrible, even to the veterans of many battles. The lines were very near each other, and from the dense underbrush and the tops of trees came puffs of smoke, the 'ping' of the bullets, and the yell of the enemy. It was a blind and bloody hunt to the death, in bewildering thickets, rather than a battle …"

The armies fought for two days. Gunfire sparked small wildfires that eventually set parts of the Wilderness on fire. Even though the combatants called cease fires to collect their wounded, many of the wounded men had burned to death or were suffocated by the smoke after the fighting ended.

At about 17,000, the number of Union casualties was more than twice that of the Confederates. By nightfall of May 6, the Union soldiers began their withdrawal. Grant pushed his men forward toward Spotsylvania Court House, which was at a crossroads on the way to Richmond. General Lee, anticipating his enemy's move, was on his way to the same spot.

THE BATTLE OF SPOTSYLVANIA

The two exhausted armies met again May 8. The fiercest fighting took place May 12 when Grant attempted a massive attack on the Confederate line. Horace Porter, an aide to General Grant, described the fight: "It was chiefly a savage hand-to-hand fight across the breastworks. Rank after rank was riddled by shot and shell and bayonet-thrusts, and finally sank, a mass of torn and mutilated corpses; then fresh troops rushed madly forward to replace the dead, and so the murderous work went on."

Union soldiers charged with bayonets at the Battle of Spotsylvania.

The battle continued until May 18, with neither side a clear-cut winner. The Union suffered about 18,000 casualties, again nearly twice the Confederate losses. The armies continued to skirmish as they moved closer to Richmond.

COLD HARBOR

The enemies clashed again May 31 at the crossroads of Cold Harbor, Virginia. The main fighting took place three days later. Grant lost more than 12,000 men over the course of the battle. About 7,000 fell in one hour.

After the defeat, Grant's army stayed at Cold Harbor until June 12. They then crossed the James River, heading for Petersburg, Virginia. When Union troops arrived in Petersburg June 15, there were only about 2,500 Confederates defending the town, although reinforcements soon arrived. Even so, the Union's three attacks failed, mainly because the commanders didn't want another slaughter like the one at Cold Harbor. They settled in for a long, siegelike campaign.

SHERMAN'S MARCH TO THE SEA

Meanwhile, General Sherman was making his way toward Atlanta. Beginning in May Sherman had chased Southern troops from Chattanooga, Tennessee, south through Georgia. The two armies fought many battles with varying results. But one thing remained constant. They continued moving closer to Atlanta, Sherman's ultimate objective.

Dissatisfied with General Johnston's continued retreating, President Jefferson Davis replaced Johnston with General John Hood. But Hood couldn't stop Sherman either. After heavy fighting in and around Atlanta, the city finally fell to Sherman's forces September 2.

General Sherman served in Missouri and Mississippi before leading the March to the Sea.

After taking Atlanta, Sherman embarked upon his famous "March to the Sea." He led about 60,000 of his troops southeast to Savannah. Sherman's troops were later blamed for burning and destroying much of the countryside. While they did burn barns that stored food supplies, deserting soldiers from both sides also contributed to the destruction.

Later in the year Sherman moved north to South Carolina. The U.S. flag flew once again over Fort Sumter on February 22, 1865. Sherman made his way north again, where Grant's men still lay entrenched around Petersburg. Meanwhile, another Union army had defeated a Confederate force in the Shenandoah Valley of Virginia.

VICTORY AT RICHMOND

Lee ordered an unsuccessful attack March 25, 1865, on the Union line at Petersburg. A Union offensive broke the Confederate line April 2 and caused the Confederates to retreat from Petersburg and evacuate Richmond. That evening the Confederate government left Richmond under the cover of darkness. The Confederate capital was now under Union control.

President Lincoln visited the city soon afterward. "Thank God I have lived to see this," he remarked. "It seems to me that I have been dreaming a horrid dream for four years, and now the nightmare is gone."

The nightmare for the soldiers hadn't quite ended, however. Grant chased Lee's army as the Confederate general searched for supplies and a way to meet up with General Joseph Johnston, who had once again taken command of what was left of the Army of Tennessee. After several costly skirmishes, Grant sent Lee a note April 7 requesting that the Army of Northern Virginia surrender. Lee responded by asking for Grant's terms of surrender. Grant replied, "I would say, that peace being my great desire, there is but one condition I would insist upon—namely, that the men and officers surrendered shall be disqualified for taking up arms again against the Government of the United States until properly exchanged."

APPOMATTOX

The armies met again April 8 in an area between Appomattox Station and Appomattox Court House in Virginia. The Confederates attempted an assault the next morning, but were quickly overcome.

Lee surrendered to Grant at the McLean home in Appomattox Court House.

The Union army had them surrounded. Lee sent a message requesting a meeting with Grant.

That afternoon Lee and Grant met at the home of Wilmer McLean in the village of Appomattox Court House. During the 90-minute meeting, the two commanders worked out the terms of surrender. The terms would be used as a model for the surrenders that soon followed throughout the Confederacy. On April 12, 1865, the Army of Northern Virginia finally laid down its arms.

After approximately 620,000 deaths and more than 1 million casualties, the Civil War was finally over. The Union had been preserved. With the ratification of the 13th Amendment to the Constitution in December 1865, slavery had ended. But it would take decades to heal the rift between the North and the South.

GRACIOUS IN VICTORY

Grant offered Lee generous terms outside of the official surrender. He ordered his officers to allow any Confederate soldiers claiming ownership of a horse to keep it. He also had three days' rations sent to the hungry soldiers.

INDEX

INTERNET SITES

Use FactHound to find Internet sites related to this book. All of the sites on FactHound have been researched by our staff.

Here's all you do:
Visit *www.facthound.com*
Type in this code: 9780756545727

GLOSSARY

ARTILLERY—large guns, such as cannons

BREASTWORK—temporary fortification during a battle

CASUALTY—person who is killed, wounded, captured, or missing during a war

CAVALRY—soldiers who fight on horseback

EMANCIPATE—to free a person or group of people from slavery

EVACUATE—to leave an area during a time of danger

GARRISON—group of soldiers based in a town and ready to defend it

INSURRECTION—act of revolting against a government

INVADE—to send armed forces into another country or area in order to take it over

PROCLAMATION—official formal public announcement

REBEL—person who fights against a government or an authority

SECEDE—to break away from a group

SIEGE—an attack designed to surround a place and cut it off from supplies or help

TREASON—act of betraying one's country

TIMELINE

1860

November 6: Abraham Lincoln is elected U.S. president

December 20: South Carolina secedes from the United States

1861

January–June: Mississippi, Florida, Alabama, Georgia, Louisiana, Texas, Virginia, Arkansas, North Carolina, and Tennessee all secede

April 12: Confederate forces attack Fort Sumter, South Carolina

July 21: Confederates win the First Battle of Bull Run

1862

April 7: Union wins the Battle of Shiloh

July 4: Confederate forces surrender at Vicksburg, Mississippi, after a siege

September 20: Confederates win the Battle of Chickamauga

November 25: Union wins the Battle of Chattanooga

1864

May 6: Confederates win the Battle of the Wilderness

May 8–19: There is no clear-cut winner at the Battle of Spotsylvania

June 12: Confederates win the Battle of Cold Harbor

September 2: Union troops capture Atlanta

December 21: Union troops occupy Savannah

June 25–July 1: Confederate army wins all but one of the Seven Days' Battles

August 30: Confederates win the Second Battle of Bull Run

September 17: Union wins the Battle of Antietam

September 22: Lincoln issues the preliminary Emancipation Proclamation

December 13: Confederates win the Battle of Fredericksburg

1863

January 1: Lincoln issues the Emancipation Proclamation

May 4: Confederates win the Battle of Chancellorsville but lose General Stonewall Jackson

July 3: Union wins the Battle of Gettysburg

1865

April 2: Confederates evacuate Petersburg and Richmond

April 9: Confederate General Robert E. Lee surrenders to Union General Ulysses S. Grant in Appomattox Court House, Virginia

April 14: President Lincoln is assassinated by John Wilkes Booth

June 23: Last Confederate troops surrender

Select Bibliography

Bearss, Edwin C. *Fields of Honor: Pivotal Battles of the Civil War.* Washington, D.C.: National Geographic Society, 2006.

Blair, Jayne E. *The Essential Civil War: A Handbook to the Battles, Armies, Navies, and Commanders.* Jefferson, N.C.: McFarland & Co., 2006.

Davis, Kenneth C. *Don't Know Much About the Civil War.* New York: William Morrow, 1996.

Hoehling, A.A. *Vicksburg: 47 Days of Siege.* Mechanicsburg, Pa.: Stackpole Books, 1996.

Hyslop, Stephen G. *Eyewitness to the Civil War: The Complete History from Secession to Reconstruction.* Washington, D.C.: National Geographic, 2006.

MacDonald, John. *Great Battles of the Civil War.* New York: Collier Books, 1992.

McPherson, James W. *Battle Cry of Freedom: The Civil War Era.* New York : Oxford University Press, 1988.

Ward, Geoffrey C., Ken Burns, and Ric Burns. *The Civil War: An Illustrated History.* New York: Knopf, 1990.

Further Reading

Baxter, Roberta. *The Southern Home Front of the Civil War.* Chicago: Heinemann Library, 2011.

Baxter, Roberta. *The Northern Home Front of the Civil War.* Chicago: Heinemann Library, 2011.

Kent, Zachary. *The Civil War: From Fort Sumter to Appomattox.* Berkeley Heights, N.J.: Enslow, 2011.

Nardo, Don. *A Nation Divided: The Long Road to the Civil War.* Mankato, Minn.: Compass Point Books, 2011.

COMPASS POINT BOOKS
a capstone imprint

Shepherd University
George Tyler Moore Center for the Study of the Civil War
Professor of History/Director
Mark Snell, PhD
CONTENT CONSULTANT:

BY STEPHANIE FITZGERALD

CONFEDERATE
PERSPECTIVE

CIVIL WAR

The Split History of the

A PERSPECTIVES
FLIP BOOK

ABOUT THE AUTHOR:

Stephanie Fitzgerald has been writing nonfiction for children for more than 10 years. Her specialties include history, wildlife, and popular culture. Stephanie is currently working on a picture book with the help of her daughter, Molly.

SOURCE NOTES:

Union Perspective

Page 6, line 11: Fordham University Modern History Sourcebook—Abraham Lincoln: First Inaugural Address, March 4, 1861. 16 April 2012. www.fordham.edu/halsall/mod/1861lincoln-aug1.asp

Page 7, line 15: Stephen G. Hyslop. *Eyewitness to the Civil War*. Washington, D.C.: National Geographic, 2006, page 73.

Page 12, line 4: Joan Waugh. *U.S. Grant: American Hero, American Myth*. Chapel Hill: University of North Carolina Press, 2009, p. 56.

Page 13, line 3: Kenneth C. Davis. *Don't Know Much about the Civil War*. New York: William Morrow, 1996, page 228.

Page 13, line 7: PBS Freedom: A History of Us—Lincoln's Generals. 16 April 2012. www.pbs.org/wnet/historyofus/web06/segment3_p.html

Page 16, sidebar, line 6: Civil War Trust—General Robert E. Lee's "Lost Order" No. 191. 16 April 2012. www.civilwar.org/education/history/primarysources/lostorder.html

Page 19, line 10: National Park Service—Fredericksburg and Spotsylvania. 16 April 2012. www.nps.gov/frsp/chist.htm

Page 23, line 10: *Don't Know Much about the Civil War*, p. 356.

Page 24, line 19: Horace Porter. "Campaigning with Grant," *The Century Illustrated Monthly Magazine* (Nov. 1896–April 1897), p. 358.

Page 27, line 18: White House Historical Association. 16 April 2012. www.whitehousehistory.org/whha_about/whitehouse_collection/whitehouse_collection-art-06.html

Page 28, line 5: U.S. Grant. *The Personal Memoirs of U.S. Grant, Volumes I and II*. Digireads.com Publishing, 2010, p. 465.

Confederate Perspective:

Page 4, line 3: *Eyewitness to the Civil War*, p. 50–51.

Page 8, line 9: Wallace Hettle. *Inventing Stonewall Jackson: A Civil War Hero in History and Memory*. Baton Rouge: Louisiana State University Press, 2011, p. 13.

Page 17, line 3: Smithsonian National Museum of American History—The Price of Freedom: Americans at War collection. 16 April 2012. www://americanhistory.si.edu/militaryhistory/collection/object.asp?ID=284

Page 19, sidebar, line 5: National Park Service—Stonewall Jackson Shrine. 16 April 2012. www.nps.gov/frsp/js.htm

Page 20, line 3: A.A. Hoehling *Vicksburg: 47 Days of Siege*, Mechanicsburg, Pa.: Stackpole Books, 1996, p. 201.

Page 28, line 1: National Archives and Records Administration—American Originals: Civil War and Reconstruction. 16 April 2012. www.archives.gov/exhibits/american_originals/civilwar.html

Table of Contents

SHARED RESOURCES

1861:

A QUEST FOR INDEPENDENCE

CH. 1

Jefferson Davis opened a telegram at his plantation near Vicksburg, Mississippi, February 10, 1861. As he read it, his wife, Varina, looked at his face. "He looked so grieved that I feared some evil had befallen our family," she said later.

The telegram said that Davis had been chosen by delegates to a meeting of the newly formed Confederate States of America to be its first president. Davis, a former U.S. senator and secretary of war, would have preferred to serve the new government in a military role, but he accepted the job of president. Seven southern states had left the Union, with four more to follow, and they needed his leadership.

After winning the Revolutionary War (1775–1783), the United States became one nation. But the former colonies were still very different, especially by region. The South's economy was based on growing staple crops, such as tobacco, rice, sugar, and most of all, cotton. The crops required a great deal of labor, which southern plantation owners filled with enslaved African-Americans.

By 1860 southern leaders were convinced that the federal government was trying to strip them of the right to pass their own laws, especially concerning slavery. The anti-slavery movement, concentrated mainly in the North, was strengthening its mission to outlaw slavery in the western territories of the country. Many anti-slavery advocates supported the new Republican political

Jefferson Davis reluctantly accepted the job of Confederate president.

The four border states were slave states that did not secede from the Union.

party. When Republican Abraham Lincoln was elected president in November 1860, the South had enough. Southern political leaders feared Lincoln and the Republicans would not stop at keeping slavery from spreading to the West. They decided to pull their states out of the Union.

South Carolina led the way, seceding December 20, 1860. In the early months of 1861, other states joined South Carolina to form the Confederacy: Alabama, Florida, Georgia, Louisiana, Mississippi, and Texas. Montgomery, Alabama, was the first capital of the Confederacy. Richmond, Virginia, became the capital in May 1861.

On April 12, 1861, Confederate soldiers fired on Fort Sumter in South Carolina, beginning the Civil War. Within a week Virginia began the process to secede. Arkansas, North Carolina, and Tennessee followed.

SETTING THE STAGE FOR WAR

When war broke out, the South had only about 18,000 factories, compared to 100,000 in the North. The South also had fewer railroad lines. These facts would prove to be major liabilities in the fight to come.

The men who held the most power in the South felt they were being bulldozed by the political and economic might of the North. As the population in northern states—and the number of free states admitted to the Union—grew, southerners felt more and more vulnerable.

Though the majority of white southerners didn't own slaves, they didn't want the government interfering in their lives. Once war was declared, the reason to fight became simple. As Union troops descended upon their homes, some southerners were moved to protect their families and property.

In April 1861 President Lincoln offered Robert E. Lee, a Virginian, command of the entire Union army. Lee was a loyal and accomplished soldier. But he was torn between duty and family. He turned down the offer and resigned his commission in the U.S. Army.

Lee would become a key figure in the Confederate army. But another commander played a starring role in the first major battle of the war. General Pierre G.T. Beauregard's army of about 22,000 men was located at a small stream called Bull Run near the town of Manassas, Virginia. The soldiers were there to keep the railroad junction from falling into enemy hands.

FIRST MANASSAS (BULL RUN)

In July 1861 Union troops under General Irvin McDowell gathered in Alexandria, Virginia. They were ready to move toward Manassas. Beauregard's men came under attack July 18, but managed to repel the enemy. McDowell attacked again July 21. As confused Confederate troops ran from the front lines, reinforcements from the Shenandoah Valley of Virginia poured in. Among them were the troops under Brigadier General Thomas J. Jackson, who refused to back down. According to legend, Confederate General Barnard Bee shouted, "Look! There is Jackson standing like a stone wall. Let us determine to die here and we will conquer! Rally behind the Virginians!" From then on, both Jackson and his brigade would be nicknamed "Stonewall." The Confederates rallied to win the battle. But their victory was hard won, with casualties of about 1,900.

General Thomas "Stonewall" Jackson (on horseback) and his brigade held off a Union assault at First Manassas.

As the South savored its victory at Manassas, the Union was determined to fight back. On February 6, 1862, Union forces seized Fort Henry on the Tennessee River. The troops, led by General Ulysses S. Grant, then captured Fort Donelson on the Cumberland River. When the forts were lost, so was access to the rivers—an important means for transporting materials and men.

General Albert Sidney Johnston, head of the Confederate army in the Western Theater, was forced to evacuate Nashville. He set out to join forces with General Beauregard at Corinth, Mississippi.

THE REALITIES OF WAR

1862

CH.2

General Albert Sidney Johnston (on horseback) was mortally wounded at Shiloh.

Meanwhile Grant set up camp at Pittsburg Landing, Tennessee, just northeast of Corinth. The camp was near a small church called Shiloh. In the early morning hours of April 6, Johnston and Beauregard launched a surprise attack.

The Confederate army drove the Union soldiers from their encampments toward the Tennessee River. By nightfall the Confederates were convinced of victory. But their triumph was marred by tragedy. General Johnston had been shot. He bled to death on the battlefield.

Things got worse for the Confederates the next morning when Grant, who had received reinforcements during the night, ordered a counterattack. This time it was the Confederates' turn to flee. The

army suffered more than 10,000 casualties. After hours of intense fighting, Beauregard led his men back to Corinth.

Later that month the Confederacy suffered another crippling defeat. A Union fleet sailed into the mouth of the Mississippi River and began a weeklong bombardment of Fort Jackson and Fort St. Philip. The two forts guarded the entrance to New Orleans. Most of Fort Jackson was destroyed, while Fort St. Philip suffered less damage because of its distance from the Union guns. The fleet steamed up the river April 24 and trained its guns on New Orleans. Union General Benjamin Butler took control of the largest city in the South—and the Confederacy's most important port.

PROTECTING THE CAPITAL

In the East, Union General George McClellan was nearing Richmond. When he saw the forces of General John Magruder at Yorktown, he thought he was outnumbered. But Magruder had no more than 13,000 men, while McClellan had about 55,000. Magruder had his men parade across the front of his lines—around and around in circles—to make their numbers seem greater than they were. Rather than attack, McClellan decided to stage a siege.

But the siege didn't happen. Instead Confederate General Joseph Johnston ordered the troops to retreat. Johnston decided to attack two Union corps located south of the Chickahominy River. The attack was scheduled for dawn May 31, but rain and miscommunication between Johnston's officers delayed it until 1 p.m. The battle took place at a crossroads called Seven Pines.

Both sides claimed victory, with the Union suffering about 5,000 casualties and the Confederates about 6,000. Near the end of the day, Johnston was shot and seriously wounded. Robert E. Lee took command of the Army of Northern Virginia.

On June 25 a skirmish broke out between Union and Confederate soldiers near woods called Oak Grove, south of Mechanicsville, Virginia. The next day General Lee launched an attack on McClellan's soldiers near Mechanicsville. The Union technically won the battle. But at the end of fighting, McClellan decided to move his position farther away from Richmond. Lee's army continued to attack for the next week. The Seven Days'

Robert E. Lee, shown at the end of the war, served as superintendent of the U.S. Military Academy before the Civil War broke out.

Battles took a harsh toll on the Confederate soldiers, with about 20,000 casualties. But Lee had managed to keep the Union army away from Richmond.

Stonewall Jackson's troops fought a battle with Union soldiers near Manassas Junction the evening of August 28. The next day Union General John Pope counterattacked. Despite heavy losses, Jackson's troops refused to yield. But Pope assumed he had won the battle and that the Confederate troops would retreat during the night.

The next day, though, General James Longstreet and his troops were on hand to reinforce Jackson's soldiers. Longstreet's men crashed into the Union lines along a 2-mile (3.2-km) front, shattering the Union army. Despite casualties of about 9,000, the victory rallied the Confederate troops.

PRESSING THE ADVANTAGE

Lee invaded the North in early September, leading his army of about 50,000 men into Maryland. The soldiers were hungry, tired—many were shoeless and lacking ammunition—and marching off to face a much greater force. But Lee knew he couldn't win the war without victory in the border states. The North had more men, more money, and more supplies.

Something happened September 13 that could have been disastrous to the Confederate army. Two Union soldiers found a copy of Lee's battle plan at an abandoned Confederate campsite near Frederick, Maryland. Armed with this information, McClellan

moved to attack the Confederates at South Mountain, but incorrectly believed his troops to be outnumbered. Even though he won the three battles at South Mountain, McClellan didn't pursue the Confederates. Lee used the time to organize his forces at Sharpsburg on the high ground west of Antietam Creek.

Fighting began at dawn September 17. The Union made three major assaults on the Confederate line. Each time Lee shifted his men to meet the attack. After a day of bloody fighting, the Union forces had pushed back the Confederates but not yet defeated them.

Despite casualties totaling about 23,000, neither side gave way. The next day both armies buried their dead and gathered the wounded. The battle became known as the "bloodiest single day in U.S. history."

General Lee led his army back across the Potomac to Virginia that evening, with Union soldiers in pursuit. Lee's troops defeated the pursuers at Shepherdstown September 20.

THE BATTLE OF FREDERICKSBURG

By November Union General Ambrose Burnside was in command of the main Union force, the Army of the Potomac. Burnside planned to march his forces on Richmond, but instead clashed with Lee at Fredericksburg, Virginia, December 13.

Lee's troops occupied high ground west of town, including a place known as Marye's Heights. Their position was at the end of an open field. For the most part, the soldiers were positioned four-deep behind a shoulder-high wall at the edge of the field.

Confederate troops prevented Union soldiers from reaching the stone wall at the base of Marye's Heights at Fredericksburg.

The morning of December 13, the first of Burnside's troops charged the wall. Confederate fire immediately cut them down. Two more brigades charged and met the same fate. Throughout the afternoon Burnside continued to send men into the firestorm. Meanwhile, Union forces temporarily broke through the Confederate line to the south, but to no avail. A truce was called December 15 so the armies could pick up their wounded and dead. The Union casualties of about 12,500 were more than twice that of the Confederate forces. Lee had handed the Union army one of the worst defeats in its history.

CH. 3
1863:
THE STRUGGLE CONTINUES

The Confederate army didn't have much time to enjoy its lopsided

victory at Fredericksburg. The winter was harsh, and the poorly

supplied troops suffered greatly. Meanwhile, many eyes turned to

the West, where Vicksburg, Mississippi, was under threat.

Early in 1863 President Lincoln named General Grant

commander of the Army of the West. Grant's orders were to take

Vicksburg, a fortress town on the eastern shore of the Mississippi

River. If Vicksburg fell, the Confederacy would physically be cut in

half. The eastern half would also be cut off from important sources

Union gunboats steamed past the Vicksburg defenses on the Mississippi River.

of supplies and men. The most important transport route in the area would be in the hands of the enemy. Jefferson Davis wasn't exaggerating when he said, "Vicksburg is the nail head that holds the South's two halves together." Throughout April southerners watched anxiously as Grant's forces pushed closer to Vicksburg.

BATTLE OF CHANCELLORSVILLE

In April 1863 Lee's Army of Northern Virginia was still entrenched at Fredericksburg. He had 60,000 men at his command—most of whom were poorly fed and clothed. By the end of the month he faced an enemy with more than twice the number of better-fed, better-equipped troops. In a battle that would come to be known

as "Lee's Masterpiece," the general quickly figured out the enemy's plan and outmaneuvered it.

General Joseph Hooker, the new commander of the Army of the Potomac, set up headquarters April 30 at a crossroads called Chancellorsville. He had 70,000 men with him. Thousands more were making their way across the Rappahannock River toward Fredericksburg. Lee quickly dispatched his cavalry, under the command of General Jeb Stuart, to take control of the roads in and out of town. Hooker had sent out most of his cavalry on a raid and therefore had no idea of what the enemy was doing.

Then Lee made a risky decision. He chose to split his army in order to attack the enemy at various positions. General Jubal Early was ordered to delay Union troops who had been deployed

General George Doles' brigade moved through the woods toward General Hooker's flank at Chancellorsville.

THE DEATH OF STONEWALL

The evening of May 2, General Stonewall Jackson and some of his officers were returning from a scouting mission when they were mistaken for a Union patrol. Jackson was hit three times by friendly fire. He died eight days later. "I have lost my right arm," said General Lee.

to Fredericksburg. Stonewall Jackson was to lead a surprise attack against Hooker's flank. The remaining 15,000 men would stage a frontal attack on Hooker's line.

Shortly before dusk May 2, Jackson's troops attacked the Union camp. It was a complete rout, with fighting that lasted two more days. But the southern victory came at a high price. The Confederate army had 13,000 casualties—about 22 percent of its total forces. The Union suffered horribly too, with about 17,000 casualties, 15 percent of its total. In addition, the Confederacy lost a beloved general—Stonewall Jackson was wounded and later died.

Despite the heavy losses suffered at Chancellorsville, the South was heartened by the victory. Lee realized that if he ever hoped to invade the North again, it was now or never. The Army of Northern Virginia started its march toward Pennsylvania June 3.

VICKSBURG UNDER SIEGE

By May Union troops had reached Vicksburg, attacking the city twice but suffering heavy casualties. Grant decided to lay siege to

the city. For six weeks Union artillery pounded Vicksburg while its trapped citizens huddled in caves and nearly starved to death. Eleven-year-old Lucy McRae wrote in her journal, "Our provisions were becoming scarce, and the Louisiana soldiers were eating rats as a delicacy, while mules were occasionally being carved up to appease the appetite. Mother would not eat mule meat, but we children ate some, and it tasted right good, having been cooked nicely."

By July the residents and soldiers could take no more. General John Pemberton, commander of Vicksburg's defenses, surrendered to General Grant July 4. The Fourth of July holiday wasn't publicly celebrated in Vicksburg again until the 1940s.

GETTYSBURG

By late June Lee's forces were in Pennsylvania. On July 1 General A.P. Hill's troops were looking for supplies near the town of Gettysburg when they clashed with Union cavalry. Two Union infantry corps soon arrived, and more Confederate infantry joined the fight. The Confederates seemed to gain the advantage, pushing the Union soldiers back toward town.

But by midnight Union reinforcements arrived by the thousands. On July 2 the fighting raged in terrible heat. Thousands of men lay dead or dying as the Confederates continued to push the enemy back and tear holes in their defenses. But at the end of the day, the Union lines still held.

The next day Lee launched what he hoped would be the decisive blow against the Union army. About 3 p.m. 12,000 troops lined

up to charge the Union line on Cemetery Ridge, led by Generals George Pickett, Johnston Pettigrew, and Isaac Trimble. They were met by artillery fire that ripped through the ranks. Still the survivors pressed on, only to be met by musket fire. After less than an hour of fighting, more than 6,000 Confederate soldiers were dead, wounded, or captured. Pickett's Charge, as it came to be known, was a failure.

The Army of Northern Virginia, which had lost a total of 28,000 men during the three-day battle, was shattered. The tide of the war had turned. Still, Lee would continue the fight for two more years.

General Lewis Armistead (top right) was mortally wounded during Pickett's Charge and died two days later.

1864-1865:

LIMPING TOWARD DEFEAT

In March 1864 General Grant was made commander of all the Union armies. His first order of business was to concentrate the Army of the Potomac and two other armies on destroying the Army of Northern Virginia. He set out toward Richmond.

Union troops crossed the Rapidan River May 4. General Lee's forces met them the next day as they attempted to pass through a thickly wooded area known as the Wilderness. Lee was outnumbered nearly two-to-one. He hoped the difficult terrain would give him an advantage that he would never have fighting in the open.

Confederate soldiers captured the Union breastworks at the Battle of the Wilderness.

The battle was completely confused—and deadly. The soldiers had to worry about more than enemy bullets. Gunfire sparked wildfires that set parts of the Wilderness ablaze. By the end of the two-day battle, Confederate casualties were around 8,000. That was less than half that of the Union losses, but the grim reality was that the Union had many more men to sacrifice to the cause.

THE BATTLE OF SPOTSYLVANIA

Lee left the battlefield and marched his troops to a strategic crossroads near Spotsylvania Court House. As Lee expected, that's where Grant's army was also headed.

The two armies clashed May 8 in a skirmish that grew into an 11-day battle. The fighting was close and fierce as Grant

General Jeb Stuart commanded the cavalry of the Army of Northern Virginia until his death following the Battle of Yellow Tavern in May 1864.

continued to move his troops left, always hoping for a break in Lee's vulnerable flank. The Confederates refused to yield. Still the two armies continued to creep closer to Richmond. And Lee continued to lose men he could not spare. One of those men was General Jeb Stuart. Stuart's death was a huge blow to Lee and the Confederacy.

The two armies met again May 31 at the crossroads of Cold Harbor, Virginia, about 10 miles (16 km) northeast of Richmond. When Grant attacked June 3, Lee's troops mowed them down by the thousands. Union casualties were about 12,000, while the Confederates lost about 2,500.

THE WAR AT HOME

Civilians in the South suffered almost as much as the soldiers during the war. Homes and fields were torn apart as fighting raged through cities and towns. Livestock was slaughtered or stolen. People lost their homes and possessions to artillery shells, fire, and enemy soldiers. All across the South people faced starvation. In 1863 the *Confederate Receipt Book* was published. The recipes in this cookbook told how to make common dishes without the necessary ingredients. A sample recipe was titled "Apple Pie without Apples."

When Grant slipped away from the battlefield, Lee assumed the general was heading for Richmond. He was mistaken. The Union soldiers were marching to Petersburg, Virginia, which was defended by only 2,500 troops. Nevertheless, the Union troops were unable to break the Confederate lines.

THE SOUTH IN FLAMES

As Grant and Lee's forces continued to clash, the Army of Tennessee faced constant harassment from General William T. Sherman's armies. That summer the Union armies fought their way from Chattanooga, Tennessee, to Atlanta, Georgia. Unhappy with the situation, President Davis replaced Confederate General

Peachtree Street was just one area of Atlanta that suffered heavy damage.

Joseph Johnston with General John Hood. He hoped Hood could stop Sherman.

By late August Hood knew Atlanta was doomed. On September 1 he ordered its citizens to evacuate. Then his troops burned everything useful to the military before abandoning the city. The Union troops took Atlanta September 2. Sherman then began his "March to the Sea" to Savannah. His troops were blamed for burning their way through the South, but both Confederate and Union deserters also caused some of the destruction.

UNDER SIEGE

In Petersburg, Virginia, the Army of Northern Virginia was still enduring siegelike conditions. The men were hungry and trapped.

Lee hastened the end of the Petersburg siege March 25 by ordering an attack on the Union line. He hoped to cause a diversion that would allow him to leave Petersburg and link up with the Army of Tennessee in North Carolina.

Lee advised President Davis to evacuate Richmond. The evening of April 2, Confederate government officials slipped out of the capital. Lee moved his army west as he tried to reach General Johnston's forces, fighting several skirmishes along the way.

On April 8 Lee gathered what was left of his ragged, hungry army between Appomattox Station and Appomattox Court House. The next morning the Confederates tried one last attack, but Union troops were closing in. Lee sadly realized he was trapped.

Petersburg, Virginia, fell to Union troops April 3, 1865.

"There is nothing left me but to go and see General Grant," he said, "and I would rather die a thousand deaths."

Lee and Grant met at the home of Wilmer McLean that afternoon to agree on the terms of surrender. The Confederate soldiers would not be charged with treason and would be allowed to keep the horses they owned. The terms would be used as a model for the surrenders that soon followed throughout the Confederacy.

The final surrender of Confederate troops took place June 23, when General Stand Watie and his Confederate Cherokee Indian forces surrendered in what is now Oklahoma. After 620,000 deaths

Wilmer McLean's home in Appomattox Court House was the site of General Lee's surrender.

and more than 1 million casualties, the Civil War was finally over. The South had lost its bid for independence.

Before the war people in the South felt at odds with those from the North because of political, economic, and social issues. After their bloody defeat, many southerners felt a bitter hatred toward their northern countrymen. In some cases it would take generations for this loathing to subside.

START TO FINISH

Wilmer McLean lived in Manassas, Virginia. In 1861 the first major battle of the Civil War took place right outside his door. McLean later moved to Appomattox Court House. In 1865 Lee surrendered to Grant inside McLean's front parlor.

INDEX